SO-EAY-719

WITHDRAWN

CELLS

CELLS

AMAZING FORMS AND FUNCTIONS

JOHN K. YOUNG

Franklin Watts
New York/London/Toronto/Sydney
A Venture Book/1990

On the cover: A photomicrograph of epithelial "goblet" cells (courtesy Carolina Biological Supply Company).

Text photos courtesy of the author

Library of Congress Cataloging-in-Publication Data

Young, John K.
Cells : amazing forms and functions / by John K. Young.
p.   cm. — (Venture book)
Includes bibliographical references.
Summary: Explores the various cells in the human body and describes how each is best suited to carry out its particular function.
ISBN 0-531-10880-5
1. Cells—Juvenile literature.   2. Cytology—Juvenile literature.
[1. Cells.]   I. Title.
QH582.5.Y68   1990
574.87—dc20
90-34262   CIP   AC

CONTENTS

ACKNOWLEDGMENTS

I would like to acknowledge my debt and gratitude for the encouragement given to me by my wife and family, by anatomists in various universities who have been my teachers and colleagues, and by many students who have continually probed and challenged my knowledge of cells.

CHAPTER ONE
WHAT IS CELL BIOLOGY?

Our current era, with its explosive increases in knowledge about the body's cells, is proving more exciting for scientists who study cells (called *histologists)* than any previous age. In fact, our time may be looked back upon as a golden age of biology. The reason for this is that the basic molecules of life can now be analyzed by new techniques of cell biology to determine their structures and roles in the cell.

This current period in cell biology, in which the basic building blocks of life are being identified, is not unlike the exciting period in physics at the turn of the century, when atoms, the building blocks of matter, were first split and analyzed. We all know the dramatic consequences of this exciting time in physics.

The effects of the ongoing explosion of information in biology still remain to be seen. In this book we present some of what cell biologists have learned about the means by which cells become so wonderfully specialized in different regions of the body, and how this knowledge has enhanced our understanding of the causes of disease.

PIONEERS IN CELL BIOLOGY

There has been speculation about the function and origin of living things for as long as we can determine: cultures and civilizations far older than our own have left behind stories and myths about the creation and functioning of humans and animals. We now know that the basic element of living things is the cell, just as the basic element of matter is the atom. But this knowledge is comparatively recent, primarily because cells are so small that they are difficult to see and examine.

The first recorded observation of cells took place in 1665 and was reported by Robert Hooke, curator of the Royal Society of London, who used one of the earliest microscopes to examine a thin slice of cork. He found that cork was composed of a honeycomb of hollow chambers that he called *cells*. What he saw, however, were only the spaces in the cork where cells once had lived. This discovery of cells was only the beginning of efforts to explain how living things function. In order to continue this quest for knowledge, at least three revolutionary advances in techniques for studying cells were necessary: 1) the invention of the light microscope; 2) the invention of the electron microscope; 3) discovery of the structure of deoxyribonucleic acid (DNA).

THE LIGHT MICROSCOPE

One of the earliest and most successful observers of cells was a Dutchman named Anton van Leeuwenhoek (1632–1723). Van Leeuwenhoek lived in a small Dutch city and made his living as a shopkeeper selling cloth and clothing. After seeing a professional glassblower at a fair, he became interested in lenses and taught himself techniques for grinding glass. At that time (1675) glass lenses were fairly common—lenses for eyeglasses had been invented as long ago as 1300 in Italy—but Van Leeuwenhoek's lenses were unusually fine and so small that they could focus on very tiny objects placed very near to the lens. During his lifetime van Leeuwenhoek manufactured some two hundred simple microscopes using these lenses and was able to see a wonderful world of tiny "animalicules" (now known as bacteria, protozoa, and sperm) that no one had ever seen before swimming freely in water. He reported his observations in many letters to contemporaries (including Robert Hooke), who reacted with astonishment, skepticism, and fascination to his descriptions of this previously unknown world. Although he never published anything like a scientific paper, and knew no languages other than his native Dutch, Van Leeuwenhoek achieved wide fame and attracted many visitors to his house eager to see his microscopic world. Perhaps his most famous visitor was the Russian tsar, Peter the Great, who was visiting Holland at the time to study shipbuilding and also wanted to see van Leeuwenhoek's tiny animals.

Strangely, relatively little progress in studying cells occurred in the hundred years or so following van Leeuwenhoek's death. It was not until 1833, for example, that Robert Brown reported the existence of the cell nucleus in plants. Subsequently (in 1839), enough knowledge had accumulated to permit the biologists Matthias Schleiden and Theodore Schwann to propose their fundamental *cell theory*, which postulated that cells are the basic units of living organisms and that all cells arise from the division of other, preexisting cells. This proposal inspired two basic questions: 1) Are infectious diseases caused by foreign cells that invade our bodies? and 2) How do the cells of our own bodies develop and function to maintain life?

ROBERT KOCH AND LOUIS PASTEUR

Study of the cells that cause disease dominated biology in the nineteenth century. Two remarkable men of that era contributed much toward an understanding of bacterial cells that cause disease. One of these was Robert Koch, a German country doctor who, after acquiring a microscope early in his practice, astonished his contemporaries by proving that a cattle disease, anthrax, was caused by a specific type of microorganism. Subsequently (in 1865), Koch was able to show which organisms caused gangrene, cholera, and tuberculosis, and borrowed items from his wife's kitchen such as potato slices and agar (animal protein) jelly that proved to be invaluable material for growing and studying microorganisms. Toward the end of his life, Koch unfortunately fell out of favor, for a number of reasons. He attempted, for example, to cure tuberculosis with an extract from killed tuberculosis bacteria called tuberculin. Tuberculin proved unable to cure tuberculosis (although it is still used in the "tuberculin test," which takes advantage of the fact that a person with tuberculosis will show a red swelling if tuberculin is injected into the skin), and when tuberculin had been accidentally contaminated with live bacteria, actually *caused* severe cases of tuberculosis.

Another giant of the nineteenth century was the French scientist Louis Pasteur. Originally a chemist, Pasteur became interested in cells and bacteria as a consequence of being approached by alcohol and wine manufacturers who wanted him to determine what was spoiling their manufacturing processes. Pasteur determined that unwanted bacteria were responsible, and that gentle heating to kill them ("pasteurization") could solve the problem. Although Pasteur made many contributions to science, his most important one was his postulation of the germ theory of disease. Pasteur and Koch were contemporaries and were acquainted with each other; unfortunately, a sense of rivalry and Pasteur's hostility to Prussia and Germans—arising from the French defeat in the Franco-Prussian War—prevented effective collaboration between these two great men.

As a result of the work of these and many other microbiologists, infectious diseases now pose a greatly reduced threat to the health of people in most parts of the world. The basic problem for medicine now, in fact, is related more closely to the cells of our own bodies. Diseases such as heart attacks, diabetes, and cancer are probably *not* due to invasion of our bodies by foreign cells but are caused by failures of our own cells to function normally. It has been much more difficult to identify the reasons for these failures, which require a detailed understanding of our cells' function. This is now the basic challenge of cell biology.

CELL SPECIALIZATION

Light microscopes have allowed scientists to find at least two hundred types of cells in the body that all look different from each other. Most of the cells in our bodies become associated with each other in specific ways to perform specific tasks. These tasks can include covering over other cells to protect them (epithelial cells), providing a structural framework for the body (bone cells and connective-tissue cells), fighting disease (cells of the immune system and the blood-stream), carrying information to other parts of the body (nerve cells and endocrine cells), providing for movement (muscle cells), and so forth. The remarkable thing about all these different cells is that all of them—and there may be as many as 100 trillion cells in the adult body!—arise from the fusion of only two germ cells, the sperm and the egg. The means by which the offspring of these germ cells become specialized to provide all these bodily functions, a basic proposal of Schleiden and Schwann's cell theory, has remained the fundamental question of all biology since these early years.

One thing that made human cells more difficult to study than bacteria was that cells in our bodies are not available as isolated, single objects that can be observed in a drop of water. Instead, they are organized into solid masses of cells that are too thick to be transparent to light and so could not be studied easily. The only way to study cells in a solid organ is to cut the organ into slices thin enough to be transparent to light.

This, however, is more easily said than done: most tissues are delicate and become torn or smashed when cut into thin sections. To avoid this, a technique was developed to replace the water in tissues with melted wax or paraffin. When the paraffin cooled, all the cell components were "frozen" in a solid block of wax. Thin sections could then be cut from this wax block more easily. In 1870 Wilhelm His invented the microtome, a machine that moved a wax block forward in very small steps. With this device, wax-embedded tissues could be cut with specially sharpened steel knives into sections so thin that their thickness was measurable in only microns. This is a very small unit of measurement—one micron is only one-thousandth of a millimeter!—so that a tissue section only five microns thick could be readily examined under the light microscope.

Now that thin, transparent sections of tissues were available, however, another problem was apparent: cells that allowed light to pass right through themselves also didn't reveal much of their structure. Somehow, a way to stain cells to make them more visible had to be devised. Early naturalists had used a variety of things, including berry juices, to stain cells. By the nineteenth century a more reliable and standardized stain was introduced by Joseph von Gerlach. This stain, lithium carmine, was actually derived from the crushed bodies of scale insects and had been discovered in antiquity by the Romans, who used it to color cloth red. By permitting the selective staining of cell nuclei, carmine was of great use to early biologists and is still used today. Another very useful stain, hematoxylin, was obtained from crushed logwood.

As the demand for stains and dyes increased in the late nineteenth century, a great variety of stains were artificially manufactured and applied to cells. The combination of all these techniques

*Microtomes are used to cut thin sections
of cells. Top: old-fashioned, sledge-type
microtome used for cutting frozen or paraffin-
embedded tissues. Tissue block (arrow) is
pushed forward toward a stainless steel
knife. Bottom: a more modern microtome used
for cutting small blocks of tissue (arrow)
embedded in plastic.*

led to a wealth of discoveries in the late nineteenth century. Among these were the identification of chromosomes as the units of heredity by Wilhelm Roux and Wilhelm Waldeyer and fundamental studies of the anatomy of cells in the nervous system by Camillo Golgi and Santiago Ramon y Cajal.

All the discoveries of the nineteenth century, using the light microscope, identified the types of cells that exist in the body and described their basic appearance. To acquire an understanding of cells' *function*, however, much more advanced techniques, involving biochemistry and electron microscopy, would be needed.

THE ELECTRON MICROSCOPE

A second revolution in the study of cell structure began in the 1930s with the invention of the electron microscope by Ernst Ruska and co-workers. The electron microscope, which illuminates tissue sections with a beam of electrons rather than with a beam of light, overcomes a basic limitation of the light microscope: cell structures smaller than about 0.2 microns in diameter cannot be seen under the light microscope. Cells range in size from about 5 to 30 microns in diameter, and many of their components are smaller than 0.2 microns and thus cannot be seen with traditional microscopy. This is because if an object is smaller than the wavelength of the light illuminating it, it will not affect the pathway of

Modern transmission electron microscope.
An electron beam projected down through
the large steel column passes through the
specimen. Magnified image is viewed through
the glass windows at the bottom.

the light, and the light ray will continue on its way as if the object weren't even there. The wavelength of an electron beam is much smaller than that of light, so much smaller cell structures can be detected. Use of the electron microscope, however, reintroduced many of the original problems that plagued the beginnings of light microscopy.

An electron beam penetrates tissue sections much more weakly than a light beam, so to be transparent to an electron beam, tissue sections must be much thinner, about 0.1 microns thick instead of 5 microns. Paraffin-embedded tissue cannot be cut this thin. Instead tissue is embedded in harder plastic resins. Also, steel knives are not sharp enough to cut such thin sections; instead knives are made of broken glass or of diamonds, which are much sharper. Tissue sections are floated on water and gently placed on metal grids that support them so that an electron beam can shine on them within a vacuum-containing chamber of an electron microscope. After the electron beam passes through the tissue section, it is projected via magnetic lenses onto either a screen or a photographic emulsion, and a highly magnified image of the cells examined is obtained.

Staining of tissues was another aspect of microscopy that had to be reinvented for use in electron microscopy. Traditional stains like carmine or hematoxylin had no effect on the passage of an electron beam and so couldn't be used to

Metal grid used for viewing tissue sections in an electron microscope. Top (low magnification): half of one grid and one plastic section of tissue, outlined by arrows, can be seen. Bottom (higher magnification): arrow points to a blood vessel containing many red blood cells, which stain darkly and have a "dumbbell" shape when cut in cross section.

stain cell components for electron microscopy. Instead tissue sections were exposed to compounds containing atoms of heavy metals such as lead or uranium. These compounds tend to stick to certain cell components and thus load these components with dense atoms of metal. These dense atoms *are* able to deflect electrons and so can be used as new stains.

All these advances have made electron microscopy a mature and routine art that is far superior to what could previously be achieved with light microscopes. The highest magnifications that early biologists could achieve with light microscopes were on the order of two-thousand-fold; now with electron microscopes, magnifications of ten thousand and fifty thousand times are routine. It has even been possible, using special preparations of biological molecules, actually to photograph the shapes of proteins and some other large molecules that compose cells. Electron microscopy has allowed the identification of numerous tiny cell components or *organelles*, that had previously been only poorly understood.

DISCOVERY OF THE STRUCTURE OF DNA

A third revolution in cell biology basically began in the 1950s and is still in full swing at the present time. This revolution began with the determination, by James Watson and Francis Crick in 1953, of the structure of DNA. Why was this discovery so important?

DNA (deoxyribonucleic acid) is extremely important to cells because it contains all the information, "written" in a sort of biological code, that is necessary to operate a cell. Each human cell contains forty-six long molecules of DNA, organized into forty-six individual chromosomes that are stored in the cell nucleus and which direct the development and function of each cell. The importance of chromosomes and genes is now the cornerstone of modern biology but has actually been known for only a short time. A roughly correct estimate of the number of chromosomes in human cells was arrived at only in 1918, and the exact number (forty-six instead of the previous estimate of forty-eight) was correctly determined only in 1956. Attempts to assign genes to individual chromosomes were first made in the 1930s, but by 1974, only about eighty-four gene loci were known.

New techniques in cell biology since then have allowed a tremendous increase in knowledge about DNA, so that more than 3,400 genes and DNA markers have now been localized to specific spots on chromosomes. This holds the promise that, for the first time, the basis of genetically inherited diseases, as well as that of diseases caused by foreign cells, can be determined. Detailed knowledge of DNA is therefore not only of interest to scientists who study cells but also has tremendous potential in medicine. This highly sophisticated knowledge about DNA took more than a century to develop.

DNA was first discovered in 1869 by Friedrich Miescher, a twenty-five-year-old researcher in the lab of a famous German chemist. One of the tasks Miescher was given was to examine the small, round cells (nowadays called lymphocytes) that accumulate in pus from infected wounds. Miescher looked at them under the microscope and found that, unlike most cells, they were composed almost entirely of a cell nucleus plus a small amount of cytoplasm. This feature allowed Miescher to break up the cells and make almost pure collections of cell nuclei. When these collections were analyzed chemically, Miescher extracted a previously unknown substance that didn't resemble proteins or any other cell components. He called it "nuclein" and spent the remainder of his career identifying the proportions of atomic elements that composed it. In 1895, at his death (hastened by overwork), Miescher was still unsure of the significance of the substance he had found.

Relatively little further progress in understanding DNA was made until the 1950s, when it was recognized that DNA and not protein was probably the portion of chromosomes that contains genes. The structure of DNA could not be determined, however, until a DNA sample pure enough to be made into crystals could be prepared. Such a preparation was analyzed in 1953 by Francis Crick, a British researcher, and James Watson, a young American who worked with Crick in Cambridge. They found that DNA is an extremely long molecule containing four different types of chemical units, arranged in a series that could be millions of different units long. It is this series of millions of different units that make up the *genetic code* of information contained in the nucleus.

How exactly is the genetic code written in DNA? DNA is composed of two long chains wrapped around each other to form a double helix. Each chain is made of alternating sugar molecules (deoxyribose) and phosphate molecules joined in a repeating sequence (diagrammed as black ribbons in fig. 1). Attached to this repeating sequence are compounds called bases (adenine, thymine, cytosine, and guanine) that are present in the interior of the helix (rectangular "keys" with rounded or pointed ends in fig. 1). The sequence of these bases in the DNA constitutes a code containing all the information needed to operate the cell.

To send a copy of this information to the rest of the cell, the DNA partially unwinds to expose a portion of the interior of the helix, and a copy of the message is made by an enzyme that assembles a chain of complementary bases into a molecule of messenger RNA (ribonucleic acid—black keys in fig. 1). Messenger RNA is similar to DNA, except that it contains only a single helix and another base, uracil, is substituted for adenine (in fig. 1, uracil is abbreviated as *u* instead of *a*).

Messenger RNA is carried outside the nucleus to small organelles called *ribosomes* (RY-bosomes). The ribosome uses the sequence of bases

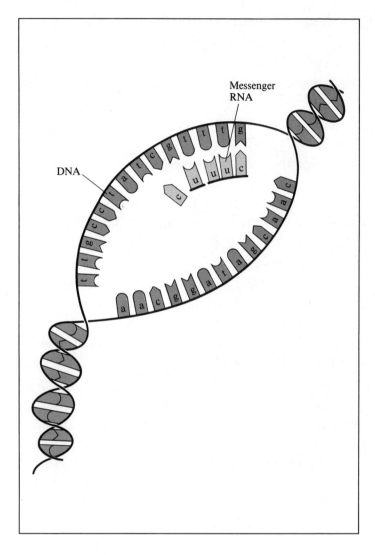

Figure 1. DNA consists of a double-helix "backbone" of deoxyribose and phosphate (black ribbons) and alternating sequences of "bases" (rectangles). Also shown is the formation of a small molecule of messenger RNA.

on the messenger RNA to assemble a long chain of amino acids. Each amino acid is "coded for" by a specific sequence of three bases on the messenger RNA. These long chains of amino acids are called *proteins*; in other words, amino acids are the building blocks of proteins. The exact sequence of amino acids, determined by the information coming from the DNA, causes each protein to take on its own unique shape and chemical properties. Each protein may thus make a specific contribution to the operation of a cell, either by helping to form the structure of the cell or by controlling chemical reactions within the cell (such proteins are called *enzymes*). The details of this genetic code were first worked out in the 1960s by Marshall Nirenberg and other scientists, who received the Nobel Prize for their work.

The proposal that millions of DNA bases contain encoded information that operates cells was both exciting and at the same time discouraging. If scientists were to examine the several thousand bases that make up a gene of interest, how in the world were they to find these bases amongst the millions of others in a chromosome? For a while this seemed to be a truly impossible task. Then, in the 1970s, three researchers—Werner Arber of Switzerland and Daniel Nathans and Hamilton Smith of the United States—were able to isolate enzymes from bacteria that cut DNA into fragments at specific, repeatable places. This allowed scientists to break up chromosomes into much smaller, manageable pieces that could easily be analyzed. Also, other bacterial enzymes allowed each piece of DNA to be inserted into bacteria, which would then grow, divide, and multiply so that millions of copies of a given piece of DNA could be produced.

All these techniques have made it much easier to analyze DNA and, as a consequence, many details of the genes responsible for the production of many proteins are now known. James Watson, one of the original investigators of DNA, has recently been appointed to direct a project that will attempt to determine the precise sequence of all the billions of bases contained in human DNA. If this is successful, the molecular explanations for all of the structures and processes within cells—the basis of life itself—will eventually become known.

CHAPTER TWO

COMMON TYPES
OF CELLS

The simplest cells in existence are those of bacteria, which are little more than membrane-enclosed containers of DNA and enzymes needed for metabolism and reproduction. Cells of such organisms, called *prokaryotes* (PRO-karee-oats), lack a cell nucleus and have DNA organized into a single loop or circle that floats within the cell in free association with enzymes, nutrients, and other molecules. The fact that these cells are very simple does not mean that they are unsuccessful —prokaryotes are found in enormous numbers all over the earth, some in environments that more complicated living things cannot tolerate. Because of their simple structure and minimal nutritional requirements, a single bacterium, dividing every twenty minutes, can produce 512 offspring in only three hours!

In spite of these successful aspects of prokaryotes, their major drawback is that they cannot combine to form complicated organisms like apple trees, ants, dogs, or human beings. Probably one reason for this is that all offspring of a bacterium look exactly the same: bacterial cells cannot specialize, or *differentiate*. Because bacterial cells cannot form specialized groups of specialized cells—in other words, organs—the tasks necessary to keep a complicated organism alive cannot be divided among different groups of cells, and nothing very complicated can be sustained.

EUKARYOTIC CELLS

The cells of most higher organisms, including both plants and animals (called *eukaryotes*, YEW-karee-oates) have quite a few features in common. Among these are a cell *nucleus*, containing long molecules of DNA organized into chromosomes, the cell *cytoplasm*, which surrounds the nucleus and which contains numerous proteins, nutrients, and organelles, and the *cell membrane*, a thin layer composed of fats (lipid) and protein that encloses the cell as a whole. Some examples of plant cells (onion root tips) are shown on p. 32. The nuclei of most of the cells are readily identifiable as grayish, circular objects (the nuclei of some of the cells lie above or below the plane of the section through the tissue, and thus are not seen). Within each nucleus, one or more dark-staining dots can often be seen. These are *nucleoli*, which are aggregations of protein and RNA that form around specific genes on one or more of the chromosomes. These genes are dedicated to the production of the RNA and proteins that form the structure of ribosomes and hence, nucleoli may be considered as little factories in the cell nucleus that produce the ribosomes.

Plant cells reproduce by means of cell division, or *mitosis* (my-TO-sis). During mitosis chromosomes greatly condense, and the two copies of each chromosome are pulled to each side of the cell so that the cell may divide and reproduce itself. The factors that control the timing and mechanisms of mitosis are not precisely known. Recently, a specific protein called *statin* has been found that appears in cells only before or after mitosis. Another protein, termed *maturation promotion factor*, appears immediately before the onset of cell division in a variety of cells and may somehow initiate mitosis. These proteins may be involved in either preventing or hastening the onset of mitosis. More study of them should reveal fundamental details about this process.

One characteristic that differentiates plant cells from other kinds of cells is a thick *cell wall* deposited on the outside of the cell membrane. These relatively thick cell walls are made of polymers of sugars and give the outlines of the cells a rather sharp and boxlike appearance. Cell walls are needed by plant cells to prevent water loss from the cell and to provide structural strength to resist dehydration. Most animals, in contrast, have complex circulatory systems that make this protection against dehydration unnecessary.

Another feature unique to plant cells is the presence of large, fluid-containing droplets or

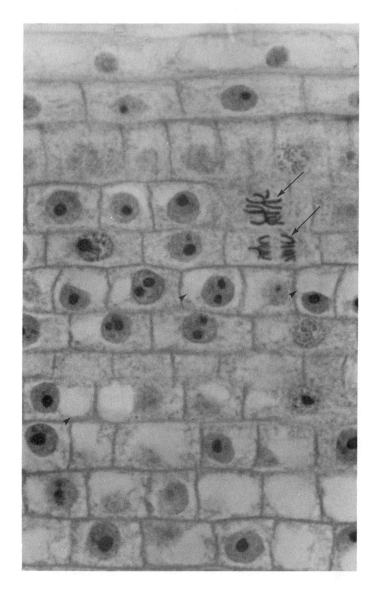

Examples of plant (onion root tip) cells.
Note mitotic chromosomes (arrows) and
fluid-containing vacuoles (arrowheads).

vacuoles that, unlike in animal cells, may account for as much as 50 percent of the volume of the cell. Once again, these vacuoles are probably related to the special regulation of water balance within plant cells. A third plant-cell specialization is the presence of small, complex organelles called *chloroplasts* that enable plant cells to use sunlight to synthesize nutrients, a process called *photosynthesis*.

ANIMAL CELLS

Substantially more information about development and specialization is known about animal cells than about plant cells. In animals, cells are usually associated with each other in specific ways to perform specific tasks. Each type of association is termed a *tissue*, and although the body may contain as many as two hundred types of cells that are all recognizably different from each other, there are only four basic ways (tissues) in which these cells may be associated. These four tissue types are:

1. Nervous tissue, containing nerve cells and glial cells
2. Muscle tissue, containing muscle cells and the blood vessels and nerves supplying the muscle
3. Epithelial tissue, composed of cells that are tightly attached to each other to cover exposed surfaces or to line hollow organs

4. Connective tissue, composed of a bewildering variety of cell types (blood cells, fat cells, fibroblasts, lymphocytes, bone cells, etc.) that "fill the spaces" in the body not occupied by nerve, muscle, or epithelia.

A brief introduction to some of the cells present in these four types of tissue will provide an idea of how variable and exquisitely specialized cells in the body are.

NERVOUS TISSUE

Hundreds of nerve cells are present in the low-magnification view of the section of nervous tissue on page 35. However, this tissue section has been prepared using a special procedure that allows only a few nerve cells to be darkly stained, so that the true shape of these cells is not obscured by the unseen tangle of nerve-cell processes that is actually present. The procedure employed to make this photo, called *immunocytochemistry*, involves using special proteins produced by cells of the immune system, called *antibodies*, as stains. Antibodies that bind (attach themselves) only to a particular enzyme present in only a portion of nerve cells were poured onto the glass slide holding the tissue section, a dye marker was attached to the antibody molecules, and the section was photographed under the microscope. This procedure has been of tremendous help to biologists because it has allowed

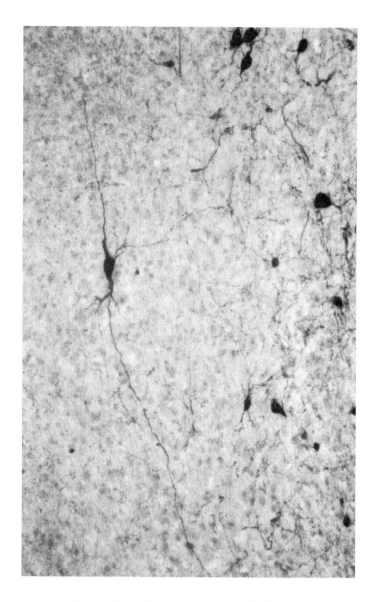

A dopaminergic neuron, stained for presence of an enzyme, tyrosine hydroxylase. The enzyme fills the entire extent of the cell.

them to determine exactly where and when specific cell proteins are present in the body. If a protein is suspected to play an important role in the development of a disease or in the function of some organ, immunocytochemistry allows scientists to examine which cells are involved.

A prominent feature of the nerve cells on page 35, like nerve cells in general, is the presence of extremely long extensions (known as *processes*) of cytoplasm leading from the central area of the cell. Called *dendrites* or *axons*, these processes carry electrical signals between the brain and the organs controlled by the nervous system. These neurons, stained by immunocytochemistry, are examples of cells containing a special protein that appear involved in the development of a disease. They contain an enzyme (named *tyrosine hydroxylase*) that synthesizes a chemical called *dopamine* from the amino acid, tyrosine. The nerve cells transport this dopamine down to the ends of long processes called axons, and when stimulated, release the dopamine from the axon terminals. Released dopamine, acting as a so-called *neurotransmitter*, activates neighboring neurons and thus allows the dopamine-containing neurons to "talk" to other neurons.

A failure of dopamine-containing neurons in a certain part of the brain to "talk" to other neurons causes a disease called *Parkinson's disease*. In this disorder the control of movement by the brain is disturbed, causing trembling of the hands and difficulty in walking. This disease gets worse with age. The cause of Parkinson's disease involves not only a failure but also the actual *death* of dopamine-containing cells, which mysteriously degenerate in Parkinson's patients but leave behind other neurons that remain healthy.

What kills dopamine-containing neurons in Parkinson's disease, and why are other types of neurons spared? Recent study suggests that some unknown environmental, toxic chemical may be involved. Further study of dopamine-containing nerve cells, using immunocytochemistry to identify them, should shed light on this disabling disorder.

A higher-magnification view of conventionally stained nerve cells is shown on page 38. The nucleoli of neurons stain particularly darkly; also, dark-staining patches present in the cytoplasm represent aggregations of membranous organelles possessing large quantities of ribosomes termed the *rough endoplasmic reticulum* (en-do-PLAZ-mik re-TIC-u-lum). These views are rather representative of most nerve cells, although, as we shall see, nerve cells may vary greatly in size and overall shape. Smaller nuclei of another type of cell (arrow) can be seen associated with the dendritic process of a neuron. These smaller cells, called *glial* (GLEE-al) *cells,* appear to protect and nourish neurons.

MUSCLE TISSUE

Another basic type of cell, the muscle cell, is very different from nerve cells. Muscle cells account for about 50 percent of the weight of our

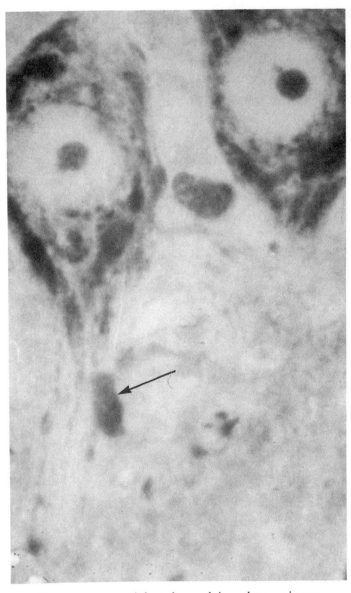

Two neurons with pale nuclei and prominent, circular nucleoli within them. Glial cells (arrow) protect and nourish neurons.

bodies and provide us with the ability to move. Three subtypes of muscle cells exist: skeletal muscle cells, which move bones; heart muscle cells, which have the remarkable ability to work virtually without rest throughout our lives and let our heart beat 86,000 times each day; and smooth muscle cells, which can adjust the diameter of hollow organs such as the gastrointestinal tract and blood vessels.

Skeletal muscle cells arise during development when immature cells line up and then fuse together, completely surrendering their individuality. This astonishing ability of cells to fuse into one very unusual structure is possessed by only a few other types of cells in the body. The mechanism and signals that initiate this fusion are still almost completely unknown. The process of fusion results in the formation of a long cylindrical structure that becomes a muscle fiber.

The outside appearance of a muscle fiber is rather unremarkable. Inside, however, the cytoplasm has a striking appearance due to the presence of large quantities of protein filaments. A high-magnification electron micrograph of a skeletal muscle fiber appears on page 40. The cytoplasm is dominated by highly ordered arrays of relatively thick protein filaments (*myosin*, arrowheads) and thinner filaments (*actin*, arrows) that are held rigidly in place in a framework composed of other newly identified proteins. The dark lines perpendicular to the actin and myosin contain these structural proteins. Contraction or

High-magnification electron micrograph of a muscle cell. Myosin fibers (arrowheads) slide against portions of actin fibers (arrows).

relaxation of a muscle fiber, and an entire muscle, takes place when the actin and myosin filaments slide back and forth against each other.

A breakthrough in the study of a crippling disease, *muscular dystrophy*, has recently come about through study of a muscle protein obtained from patients suffering from this disorder. This new protein, termed *dystrophin*, appears to connect the actin and myosin to the cell membrane of the muscle fiber. Improper production of this protein leads to abnormalities in muscle contraction and may be the basis for muscular dystrophy. Perhaps this new understanding of the molecular basis of muscular dystrophy will lead to better methods of treatment.

EPITHELIAL AND CONNECTIVE TISSUES

Epithelial cells can be joined together to perform at least two tasks. One such task, to protect underlying cells from friction, chemicals, or dehydration, is a particularly prominent job for cells of the skin or for cells lining the digestive system. Another task of epithelial cells is to form hollow sacs that make up the bulk of glandular organs. Some glands, called *exocrine* (EKS-o-krin) glands, have hollow sacs that all connect to ducts; the epithelial cells that form these sacs produce proteins that are carried via the ducts to another organ. Other glands, called *endocrine* (EN-do-krin) glands, are formed from epithelial cells that secrete proteins directly into blood vessels. In this latter case the proteins are free to be carried and to act all over the body, and they are defined as *hormones.*

Some typical examples of endocrine epithelial cells can be found in hollow structures located in the thyroid gland called thyroid follicles. These follicles contain a stored form of the hormone produced by the thyroid gland. This stored form of hormone is secreted by the epithelial cells forming the follicle. These cells have round nuclei and a rectangular overall shape. Not all epithelial cells in the body have this shape—they can be much flatter, as in blood vessels, or much taller—but like all epithelial cells, they are tightly bound together by specialized structures in their cell membranes called *cell junctions.*

The photo on page 43 also shows some connective tissue cells (arrows) in the spaces between the follicles. The types of cells present in connective tissue are so numerous and varied that a description of them would involve a very lengthy list. However, one feature in common is that they all can secrete a variety of substances into their environment, and they all may be widely separated from other cells at some point in their lives.

SPERM AND EGG CELLS

One final type of cell that does not easily fit into these four categories is the germ cell, or *gamete.*

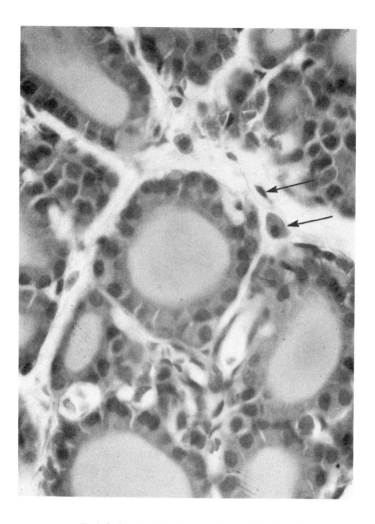

Epithelial cells in the thyroid gland enclose hollow cavities (follicles). These cavities are filled with a fluid (pale gray central areas) that contains a stored form of thyroid hormone. Arrows: connective tissue cells (probably a mast cell and a fibroblast) that inhabit the areas between follicles.

Germ cells (sperm and egg cells) are produced by a special variant of mitosis, termed *meiosis* (my-O-sis), which results in cells possessing only one set of chromosomes instead of the normal two. As a result, when the cells fuse together during sexual reproduction, sets of chromosomes from both parents can be combined to form the normal complement of chromosomes in the body cells of a baby. This constant recombination of genetic material appears to be a major factor in the evolution of such an enormous diversity of higher organisms on earth.

CHAPTER THREE
SPECIALIZED ORGANELLES AND MOLECULES

We have looked at a number of cells that had very different shapes and functions. Yet, basically, these cells still had much in common with each other: they all had regularly shaped nuclei with a normal number of chromosomes, they all had a "normal" complement of intracellular organelles, and all could in many ways be considered typical cells.

In the next three chapters we'll consider unusual, even bizarre cells that don't conform to these normal characteristics. These cells are interesting precisely because they *don't* conform to the standard view of the cell and thus challenge conventional thinking on which organelles and molecules a cell needs to survive and be normal. As we shall see, cells will take extraordinary measures to fulfill their assigned tasks, which often are essential for the survival of the body as a whole.

THE MEGAKARYOCYTE

One of the most peculiar cells in the body is the *megakaryocyte* (mega-KAR-i-o-site), a cell that clings to the outside of blood vessels that pass through cell-filled cavities within hollow bones. Cells within these bony chambers are called *bone marrow cells* and, since they are devoted to the production of blood cells, are classified as *connective tissue cells*. A megakaryocyte is a special type of bone marrow cell (fig. 2). These cells are enormous, with a diameter as much as ten-fold greater than that of most cells. They have a bizarre-looking, swollen cell nucleus that often contains *sixteen times* more DNA than nuclei of other cells. The overall shape of these cells is also peculiar: megakaryocytes extend long, tentacle-like processes into the interior of blood vessels that they cling to; once these processes penetrate into the blood vessel, the cell allows them to break into pieces and shed portions of cytoplasm from the tip of each process. As it turns out, these fragments of megakaryocytes are useful to the body: they become *platelets*, small cell fragments that regulate blood clotting and blood vessel repair.

It's very comforting that the unusual appearance and behavior of these cells can at least be related to a useful function. A little thinking about these cells, however, raises a lot of puzzling questions. Why do these cells have to be so big? Why do they have so much DNA, and what

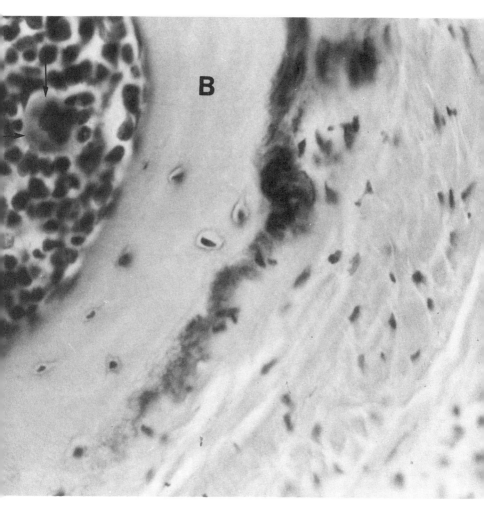

B

Cross section through a hollow bone.
Shown are the outer layer of bone (B)
and masses of dark-staining bone marrow
cells in the interior. A megakaryocyte
(arrows) is identifiable by its large
size and misshapen nucleus.

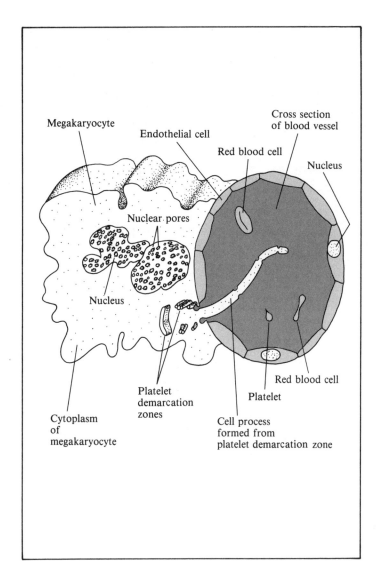

Figure 2. A megakaryocyte. Note the distorted nucleus, the cytoplasmic "tentacles" that will be divided into platelets, and the hollow spaces within the cytoplasm called platelet demarcation zones.

makes their nuclei so misshapen? How do these cells "know" how to attach to a blood vessel, and how do they even "know" that the blood vessel is present at all? How can a cell distort its cell membrane to make their tentaclelike processes, and how can a cell permit pieces of itself to be broken off? How do the chemicals present in platelets come to be located at the ends of the tentacles? And finally, what could stimulate a cell to develop into such a monster?

In fig. 3, the basic features of a relatively undifferentiated epithelial cell, like those that may be found in the respiratory or digestive organs of an early embryo, are diagrammed. The most prominent features of this cell are an outermost cell membrane (A), various organelles, and a central, spherical cell nucleus, which can all be examined one by one.

THE CELL MEMBRANE

Great strides have been made in understanding the structure of the cell membrane in recent years. It is partly composed of a thin film of fatty lipid molecules—basically, long chains of carbon atoms—that form a watertight envelope around the cell. This film is very fluid, not unlike a layer of kerosene upon a drop of water, so that, more than anything else, the lipid component of the cell membrane resembles the film of soap on a soap bubble.

Several varieties of proteins are visible in fig. 3B. Some of these proteins are constructed to provide pores or channels through the membrane that allow the passage of small, water soluble molecules that otherwise could not penetrate the lipid barrier. In fig. 3C, for example, the membrane-associated glucose-transporter protein is represented as a cylindrical molecule with a central pore.

In reality, this protein is not a cylinder but a long chain of 470 amino acids with a molecule of NH_2 located at one end of the chain and a molecule of COOH at the other end. In twelve places, which are each tightly coiled into a helix, the protein passes right through the plasma membrane, forms a loop on the other side, and then passes through the membrane again to reenter the cytoplasmic portion of the cell (see expanded diagram at the top of the figure). The consequence of this is that the protein forms a ring which is analogous to a piece of yarn stitched onto a sheet of cardboard to form a circle. Through the center of the ring, the sugar glucose is taken into the cell to provide nourishment: enzymes break up the glucose into smaller molecules, which are then sent to *mitochondria* to be completely combined with oxygen, providing energy to operate the cell.

Current research on the glucose-transporter protein involves examining it for abnormalities in patients with a disease called *diabetes mellitus.* In this disease cells fail to take up glucose from the bloodstream in response to a hormone called *insulin.* As a result, glucose levels become very high in the bloodstream and damage structures

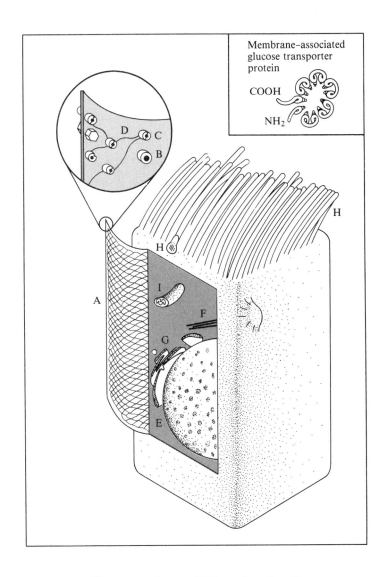

Figure 3. An undifferentiated cell.

(A) Cell membrane. (B-D) Network of proteins associated with the cell membrane. (E) Nucleus. Also shown are (F) actin and myosin (G) Golgi body, (H) basal body of cilium (made of microtubules), and (I) mitochondrion. The structure of the membrane-associated glucose transporter protein (C) is enlarged in the upper right-hand corner.

in the eye, blood vessels, and kidney. More study of this glucose-transporter protein may perhaps reveal what the problem is in diabetes mellitus.

Another transport channel (D) is formed when two identical molecules of the so-called *band 3 protein* come together. This protein also has membrane-piercing helices, but each protein forms only a semicircle, so that two molecules are needed to complete the channel. Substances passing through this channel include water, bicarbonate, and a few other ions. Work done on membranes from red blood cells indicates that band 3 proteins are connected together by thin filamentous proteins (spectrin) to form a vast undulating network of proteins on the inner surface of the cell membrane. This network seems to be the structure that gives each cell its own special and relatively rigid shape; without it, all cells would resemble delicate, balloon-shaped spheres.

A number of other long, rigid protein molecules can attach to the cell membrane and project into the cytoplasm. Among these are actin and myosin (fig. 3F), proteins that are incredibly abundant in muscle cells but which are also present in many other cell types. These protein fibers can generate force by sliding against each other. In this way the surface of the cell can be deformed to change the overall shape of the cell or to exert pressure upon neighboring cells.

An interaction of all these membrane-associated proteins very likely explains how a megakaryocyte can change its shape so drastically.

The steps involved in producing a megakaryocyte "tentacle" have recently been worked out (See fig. 2). First, the cell membrane folds in on itself to produce a hollow, sausage-shaped bubble. Then a series of these bubbles is produced and arranged side to side so that they may be fused into a large, flattened, empty space called a *platelet demarcation zone*. Finally, a large area of cytoplasm is surrounded on all sides by several of these demarcation zones so that it can be separated from the rest of the cytoplasm and pushed toward the surface of the cell as a "tentacle." What remains to be explained is how membrane-associated proteins are coordinated to produce all these changes at the right places and times.

Additional cell-membrane proteins, represented as hexagons in fig. 3, are receptor proteins that can attach to specific molecules present in the environment around the cell. Without actually entering the cell, these receptor molecules allow it to "sense" changes in the types of molecules around it. An interaction of these receptor-type proteins with proteins associated with blood vessels is probably one way a megakaryocyte can "sense" the presence of a nearby blood vessel and attach itself to it.

THE CELL NUCLEUS: COMMAND CENTER

The cell nucleus is the repository of all the genetic material (DNA) needed to operate the cell. It is an unusual cell component in that it is enclosed by two membranous layers rather than one, which are separated by a fluid-filled space, the *perinuclear cisterna* (fig. 4). Ribosomes can often be observed attached to the outermost membrane of the nuclear envelope. In fig. 4 ribosomes are represented as dark, figure-eight shaped structures, which illustrates the principle that ribosomes actively engaged in producing a protein are composed of two different-sized subunits.

The small and large subunits of a ribosome, in turn, are composed of twenty-one and thirty-four different proteins, respectively, plus large amounts of a special type of RNA called ribosomal RNA. Since ribosomes are so small, up to now it has been difficult to determine their exact shape and how exactly all these proteins and RNA are put together. Ribosomes bind to the outer nuclear membrane because this membrane possesses a binding protein, *ribophorin*, that allows them to attach and inject their manufactured amino acid chains into the perinuclear cistern.

As mentioned above, the subunits for ribosomes are some of the few things that are actually constructed inside the nucleus, by genes and proteins located inside the nucleolus. How do these subunits get out of the nucleus and into the cytoplasm? It is believed that they are somehow guided out of the nucleus through holes in the nuclear envelope called *nuclear pores*. These nuclear pores are composed of a ring of eight globular protein subunits that are gathered around

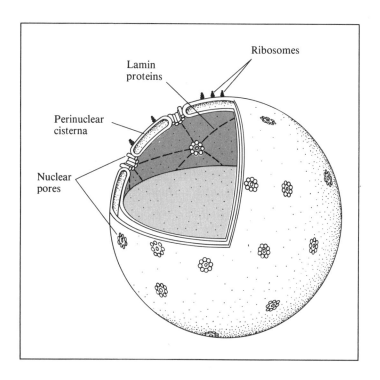

Figure 4. A cell nucleus, showing nuclear pores, ribosomes, and the network of interconnected lamin proteins on the inner surface of the nuclear envelope.

a ninth protein "plug." In addition to ribosomal subunits, nuclear pores allow the passage of messenger RNA molecules into the cytoplasm and thus provide for the control of the cytoplasm by the nucleus. The nuclear pores are all connected to each other by a network of proteins called *lamins* (dashed lines in fig. 4). It is this network of nuclear pores connected by lamins that gives the nucleus of any given cell type its strength and special shape. Megakaryocytes are no exception to this rule, so some alteration in the function of the nuclear lamin proteins must be involved in producing the peculiar shape of the nucleus in megakaryocytes.

It is the contents of the nucleus, the chromosomes, that are of particular interest to a biologist. Chromosomes are composed of DNA plus proteins that organize the DNA into a chromosomal shape and which regulate those portions of the DNA that are activated to make the proteins characteristic of a given type of cell. Organization of the DNA alone is a terrific accomplishment: if the DNA molecules of a given cell were placed end to end, you would get a narrow thread of DNA almost three feet long! Details of the way in which all this DNA is packaged without getting tangled are only now becoming known. It is still a mystery why megakaryocytes make so much DNA; perhaps more is necessary to synthesize the proteins needed to control such an enormous volume of cytoplasm.

The DNA of most cells has a number of mysterious features. Theoretically, there is enough information coded into a cell's DNA to make millions of different proteins. However, only about 1 to 2 percent of a given cell's DNA is actually transcribed into messenger RNA to make proteins. The amount of active DNA indicates that cells at most make 80,000 to 100,000 proteins. This may seem like a lot but actually is so much less than the potential number that it offers the hope that eventually *all* of a cell's proteins can be understood. If so little DNA is involved in protein production, what can be the function of the remaining 95 percent of the DNA? A further mystery arises from the fact that about 25 percent of a cell's DNA represents sequences of 100 to 1000 bases that may be repeated hundreds, or even thousands, of times. What is the function of this enormous amount of highly repetitive DNA? New knowledge of nuclear DNA has presented at least as many questions as answers.

CYTOPLASM PROTEINS

A variety of protein fibers, known as *cytoskeletal proteins*, fill the cytoplasm of cells and contribute to their structure. Some of these, such as actin and myosin (F, fig. 3), can generate movement by sliding against each other and by allowing cells to deform their shape or to exert pressure upon other cells; this function is exaggerated to a remarkable degree in muscle cells, as we have seen. Other proteins, termed *intermediate filaments* (a common type is made of a protein called *keratin)* form a tough, interconnected network within the cytoplasm that holds things in place: for example, numerous intermediate filaments are connected to both nuclear pores and to sites on the cell membrane and apparently anchor the nucleus in place within the cytoplasm.

MEMBRANOUS ORGANELLES: ENDOPLASMIC RETICULUM AND GOLGI APPARATUS

A cell's cytoplasm contains a number of membranes that are organized either into hollow, flattened sacs (fig. 3G) or into a network of interconnected, hollow tubules. The proteins that are responsible for the distinctive shapes of these membranous organelles are not now known. A portion of these membranes will have ribosomes attached, and because of the resultant dotted appearance in electron micrographs are called *rough endoplasmic reticulum.* Ribosomes settle onto the surface of endoplasmic reticulum only when they manufacture a protein designed to be inserted into a membrane or packaged for export out of the cell. Such a protein will have a distinctive sequence of amino acids at its beginning called a *signal sequence.*

This signal sequence, as soon as it is made by the ribosome, attracts a cytoplasmic component called the *signal recognition particle* that attaches to the protein as it is still being made and drags the protein plus the attached ribosome down onto the surface of the endoplasmic reticulum. The signal sequence of the protein is then threaded into the membrane of the endoplasmic reticulum, so that the protein either will be stuck into that membrane or will pass completely through it into the cavity within the endoplasmic reticulum. In megakaryocytes the rough endoplasmic reticulum is highly active in making the proteins and chemicals that will be transported to parts of the cell that will become platelets. Transport of proteins away from the endoplasmic reticulum takes place in several steps. First, portions of the endoplasmic reticulum bud off, forming little vesicles that transport the newly made protein to another membranous organelle, the *Golgi apparatus.* After additional modification in the Golgi apparatus (e.g., sugar molecules may be attached to proteins at this time), more vesicles will carry the protein to the cell surface, where they may be anchored into the cell membrane or secreted into the environment around the cell.

MITOCHONDRIA: POWER PLANTS OF THE CELL

Mitochondria (fig. 3I) are other examples of membranous organelles. Mitochondria are the sites where small fragments of sugars and other nutrients are completely burned, that is, combined with oxygen, to extract the maximal amount of energy from them. This is accomplished in a series of ingenious steps that slowly release the energy in nutrients. If this energy were to be released quickly—that is, if the nutrients actually *were* burned—cells would be damaged.

Mitochondria may be quite numerous—a cell may possess several hundred of them—and have been seen to "swim" vigorously around the cytoplasm and frequently change their shape. The means and reasons for this odd and fascinating behavior of mitochondria are still not known. Mitochondria are distinctive in having *two* membrane layers, the inner one highly folded and chemically very different from other cell membranes.

During this process of energy release, the carbon atoms of a carbohydrate molecule are combined with oxygen in the interior of a mitochondrion to form carbon dioxide, while the hydrogen ions (H+) are stripped off of the carbohydrate. These H+ ions are carried toward the outer membrane of the mitochondrion, using energy provided by the reaction of the carbohydrate with oxygen. As a consequence, a strong positive charge forms between the inner and outer membranes of a mitochondrion. Just as in a battery, there is a vigorous tendency for ions to flow toward each other to correct this separation of charge, and the mitochondrion takes advantage of this tendency to produce energy. All the H+ ions rush back into the innermost core of the mitochondrion through channels formed by a special protein. This protein uses the energy in this flow of H+ ions to generate a high-energy molecule called adenosine triphosphate *(ATP)*.

This whole process of extracting the energy from a flow of H+ ions is not unlike the way in which a waterwheel would extract the energy from a flow of water in a generating plant. The ATP made by mitochondria can be carried throughout the cell and can be used to activate enzymes involved in a great variety of cell functions.

Besides being the only place in the cell where the maximal amount of energy can be extracted from nutrients, mitochondria have one other feature that sets them apart. This feature is a small amount of DNA that is arranged into a circular loop, just as in bacteria. Why should mitochondria have their own DNA? Some have speculated that mitochondria actually originated as free-living, independent bacteria that were "eaten" by primitive cells millions of years ago.

CILIA

Cilia are tubular projections of the cell membrane that are supported on the inside by a rigid arrangement of *microtubules*. The *basal body* of a cilium, containing microtubules, is shown in fig. 3H. Some cells possess dozens or hundreds of cilia, such as cells in the respiratory tract, which use the cilia to propel a protective coat of mucus up toward the pharynx by causing the cilia to wave back and forth. Many other cells, however, have only one to two cilia that don't move. In these cases—e.g., with bone cells, cartilage cells, contractile cells of glands, sodium-sensing cells of the kidney, odor-sensing cells of the nose—the cilia may somehow act as sensors and allow the cells to respond to changes in their environment.

The basic structural element of each cilium

is formed by microtubules that are arranged into nine parallel microtubule doublets surrounding a central pair of microtubules that together constitute a cylindrical structure called an *axoneme* (fig. 5). All the microtubule doublets are connected to each other by elastic protein links called *nexins;* as a result, the doublets are not entirely free to slide past each other, so that any sliding results in a bending of the axoneme and a waving of the cilium. All the microtubules in a cilium, in turn, are composed of particles formed by the association of two molecules of a protein called *tubulin,* which spontaneously assemble into microtubules at the right temperature, concentration, and pH.

Cilia are not the only places in the cell where microtubules are located. As a matter of fact, strands of microtubules stream through the cytoplasm in many places and may act as "railroad tracks" for the transport of organelles and other things throughout the cell. When an organelle such as a mitochondrion is transported on this "rail system," the organelle first attaches to a "motor protein" such as *dynein* (DY-neen) or *kinesin* (ky-NEE-sin). This motor protein then has the ability to move rapidly along a microtubule, dragging the organelle with it and using ATP for energy along the way. At the end of the trip, the organelle is detached from the motor protein and takes up residence in another part of the cell. In megakaryocytes, vesicles containing proteins "addressed" to parts of the cell

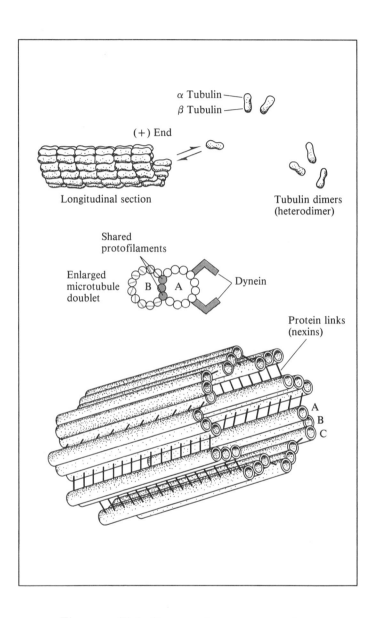

Figure 5. Tubulin proteins aggregate into microtubules that are then assembled into a complicated structure called an axoneme.

that will become platelets are probably sent via this microtubule railroad system.

Another important example of the involvement of microtubules in intracellular transport is seen during mitosis, when microtubules originating at structures called *centrioles* line up to form structures that organize the movement of the condensed chromosomes. A better understanding of how the microtubular transport system is organized and coordinated would provide many clues as to how the lives of cells are maintained.

From all of the above, it seems that cells possess many of the features present in larger organisms. They have bones and muscles (actin-myosin -intermediate filaments), skin (cell membrane), a digestive system (mitochondria), and a circulatory system (transport vesicles, Golgi apparatus, microtubules). All of these organelles and molecules within the cell are probably involved in giving megakaryocytes the peculiar features we have puzzled over. One question, however, hasn't been addressed yet: what makes a bone marrow cell turn into a megakaryocyte in the first place?

Two protein *hormones* have been extracted from blood that are both involved in transforming certain marrow cells into megakaryocytes. One of these is called *megakaryocyte colony stimulating factor* and is a protein composed of about fifteen hundred amino acids. Nothing is known thus far about where this hormone comes from in the body. The other hormone affecting mega-karyocytes is called *thrombopoietin* (throm-bo-PO-ee-tin) and is made up of about three hundred amino acids. Curiously, this hormone appears to be made by cells in the kidney, which seem to constantly monitor the blood in some way to make sure that blood contains the proper amount of various substances. If the number of platelets in the blood were to fall drastically, blood would not clot properly, and a person would be in danger of bleeding to death from a simple cut! Somehow, kidney cells can sense when there are not enough platelets in the blood, and secrete thrombopoietin to stimulate cells in the bone marrow and correct the situation.

All the information presented above shows how the tools and novel findings of cell biology can at least partly be used to explain how even a bizarre cell like a megakaryocyte takes on its appearance and function. Even so, a lot more basic information is still unknown. The events within cells that specifically cause the appearance of a mature megakaryocyte remain a virtual mystery. How are the "megakaryocyte" genes selectively activated and identified in the DNA? How are unneeded genes "turned off?" A look at other unusual cells in the body may perhaps give us a clearer view of what needs to be accomplished to explain the cell theory truly.

CHAPTER FOUR
SOME UNUSUAL EPITHELIAL CELLS

Many epithelial cells (cells that cover exposed surfaces and line hollow organs) appear different from each other and can be tall and thin, round, or flat. Some epithelial cells, however, take on such bizarre shapes that scientists have wondered how they can acquire and survive such changes. Here are a few examples of strange epithelial cells.

LENS CELLS

If megakaryocytes appeared peculiar because of their complexity, then lens cells are strange because they are so *simple*. Lens cells are extremely long cells that are stacked upon one another in the lens of the eye. They are hexagonal in cross section (see fig. 6) and have a cytoplasm that is noteworthy for the *lack* of things seen in most cells. Lens cells (also called *lens fibers* because of their length) often have no ribosomes, no mem-

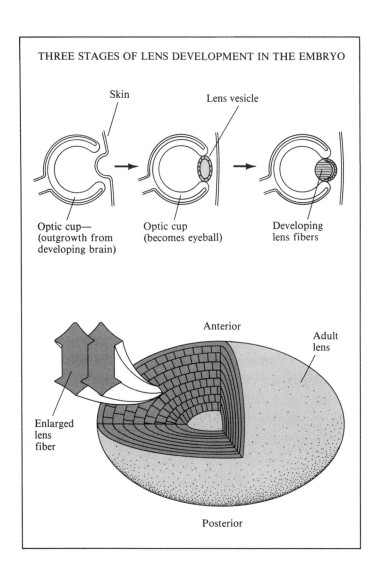

THREE STAGES OF LENS DEVELOPMENT IN THE EMBRYO

Skin

Lens vesicle

Optic cup—
(outgrowth from
developing brain)

Optic cup
(becomes eyeball)

Developing
lens fibers

Anterior

Adult
lens

Enlarged
lens
fiber

Posterior

*Figure 6. Lens cells arise during develop-
ment when epithelial cells in the posterior
portion of the lens become very long and
fill in the cavity within the developing lens.*

branous organelles like mitochondria or endoplasmic reticulum, and no nucleus! Why is this, and how can a cell survive without these things? Are these cells really alive?

The reason lens cells lack organelles probably is related to their job: transmitting and bending rays of light entering the eye. Large objects like organelles would interfere with the transparency of these cells and so have been dispensed with. Most of the cytoplasm is instead filled with filaments of proteins called *crystallins*, which are so regularly ordered in space (much like silicon atoms in a piece of quartz) that they permit the passage of light. Lens cells can survive because they *do* possess enzymes allowing the partial metabolism of glucose and other nutrients, in the absence of mitochondria and reactions with oxygen, that provide some energy.

The simplicity of the structure of lens cells does, however, cause quite a few problems. One problem relates to turnover of proteins. Most cell proteins are present only temporarily in cells, being degraded by enzymes within two to five days so that they can be replaced by new proteins. Lens fibers, lacking nuclei or endoplasmic reticulum, are unable to degrade or replace crystallins, so that molecules of crystallin remain in place for the life of each cell (decades, if not longer!). Over the course of the years, each protein molecule may undergo chemical reactions with glucose or other molecules present within the eyeball, so that gradually the crystallins may become deformed or adherent to each other. This may result in the loss of lens transparency known as *cataract.*

Accumulation of abnormal proteins within lens cells may not only lead to cataract but could actually result in lens cells being attacked and killed by cells of the immune system. Abnormal cell proteins often are no longer recognized as belonging to the body by cells of the immune system and can provoke a reaction by immune system cells called macrophages. Fortunately for lens cells, macrophages and other cells cannot gain access to the interior of the eye and the fluid within *(aqueous humor)* because blood vessels in the wall of the eyeball are specialized to block any blood or immune cells from leaving the vessel and entering the aqueous humor.

Another problem arises from the lack of blood vessels within the lens. The cells within the center of the lens are many millimeters away from the oxygen-and nutrient-rich fluid that bathes the lens of the eye within the eyeball. Nutrients cannot possibly diffuse passively across all these cells without being carried by blood vessels, so why don't the innermost lens cells starve to death? The solution to this problem probably relates to the origin of lens cells as specialized epithelial cells. As noted previously, epithelial cells are usually tightly connected to each other by structures called *cell junctions.* One type of cell junction is called a *communicating junction* because the membrane proteins that form it create small channels that connect the cytoplasm of one cell with that of its neighbor. Nutrients can be passed from one cell to another via these junctions, thus saving the lives of the lens cells buried in the interior of the lens.

Lens development is diagrammed at the top of fig. 6. In the embryo, the retinal portion of the eye forms as a spherical outgrowth of the brain called the *optic cup*. When the optic cup reaches the developing cornea, it causes a portion of it to grow inward and pinch off, forming a hollow *lens vesicle* composed of an inner, hollow cavity and an outer layer of tall epithelial cells. With time, the posterior layer of epithelial cells becomes taller and taller, obliterating the hollow cavity and eventually coming to make up most of the lens. At the same time these epithelial cells lose their organelles.

PODOCYTES

Other peculiar epithelial cells, found in the kidney, are called *podocytes* (PO-do-sites). Like megakaryocytes, these cells also cling to capillaries but have an entirely different job: their function is to filter the fluid that leaks out of the capillaries and to produce urine. This is not quite as simple a task as it may seem. Podocytes must let fluid out of the capillaries but at the same time prevent blood cells and valuable proteins from escaping and being lost from the body in the urine. Special features of podocytes allow them to accomplish this.

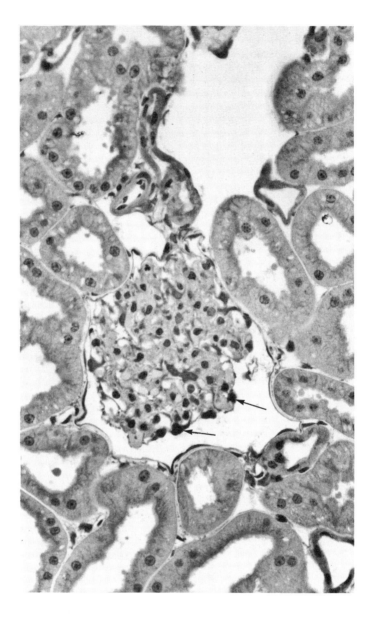

*Renal glomerulus. Dark cells (arrows)
are podocytes covering over the knot
of glomerular capillaries.*

Podocytes are found clinging to specialized groups or "knots" of capillaries in the kidney called *glomeruli* (glo-MER-u-li). Each kidney may contain as many as *two million* glomeruli, which are formed from unusually "leaky" capillaries enclosed by a layer of podocytes, a fluid-filled cavity, and finally by a third layer of more ordinary epithelial cells (see fig. 7). Fluid that passes through the capillary wall and the layer of podocytes accumulates in the space between the epithelial layers and travels away from the glomerulus through a series of tubules that eventually lead to the urinary bladder. Each podocyte settles down on a capillary like an octopus, throwing many "arms" around the capillary and interlocking these arms with those of other podocytes. Each arm itself extends many tiny processes called *foot processes* (these give the cell its name— *podocyte* means "foot cell" in Latin) that densely cover the surface of each capillary. The only way fluid can escape from the capillary is via tiny, slitlike spaces between the foot processes, appropriately called *filtration slits.*

Once again, the same questions that came to mind about megakaryocytes can also be asked about podocytes. How does the cell "know" that a capillary is nearby to attach to, and what makes it develop such elaborate processes?

The way that podocytes attach to capillaries is now known. First, podocytes are not directly connected to the capillary wall itself. Instead the cells attach to a thin, jellylike layer called a *basal*

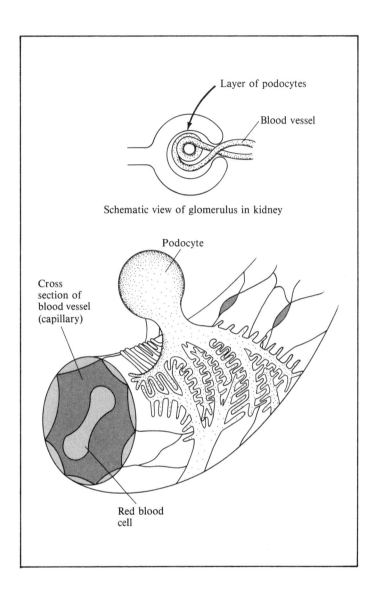

Layer of podocytes

Blood vessel

Schematic view of glomerulus in kidney

Podocyte

Cross
section of
blood vessel
(capillary)

Red blood
cell

*Figure 7. Podocytes in the kidney.
Note the long cell processes that wrap
around a capillary and filter the fluid
leaking out to produce urine.*

lamina composed of protein *(type IV collagen)* (COL-a-gen) and carbohydrates, which is sandwiched between the capillary and the podocytes. A basal lamina is very often found beneath many epithelial cells. In the kidney glomeruli, it acts like an additional filter to prevent small, charged proteins from entering the urine. Another protein, named *fibronectin* (fi-bro-NEK-tin) "glues" the podocyte to the basal lamina by acting as a link connecting the collagen in the basal lamina with receptors in the podocyte cell membrane. This is probably how both podocytes and megakaryocytes "know" how to attach themselves to capillaries: when their cell-membrane receptors attach to the fibronectin and collagen wrapped around a capillary, the cells change their shape and become associated with the capillary, too.

What makes podocytes acquire their unusual shape? Only a few steps in podocyte development are understood. The first step is the formation of hollow balls of epithelial cells in the embryonic kidney. The substance that seems to trigger this is, of all things, *iron.* Iron atoms appear to be carried to the developing kidney by a carrier protein named *transferrin* (trans-FAIR-in). This carrier protein attaches to transferrin receptors on the cell membrane and somehow enables iron to enter the cell.

Once inside, iron apparently alters the function of DNA, causing balls of epithelial cells to form. These epithelial cells then produce another protein called an *angiogenesis* (an-gi-o-GEN-e-sis) *factor,* which causes capillaries to grow toward the epithelial balls. When a capillary touches one of these epithelial balls, the cells it touches are transformed into podocytes. This is only one of many examples of contact between two cell types that causes a change in development, but the mechanism of this almost miraculous effect is still not known.

An influence of iron atoms upon development is not limited to the kidney: iron deposited upon a growing muscle by nerve cells causes a permanent change in the contractile properties of that muscle, and iron in the bone marrow influences the development of blood cells. The way these metal atoms can affect the function of DNA in such a precise and effective manner is also still a mystery. Thus, while some reasons for the development of peculiar cells like podocytes are known, there is still a lot of unknown territory to explore in developmental biology.

THYMIC NURSE CELLS

Most histologists would probably agree that the strangest cells in the body are the so-called *thymic nurse cells* that have recently been found in the thymus. Many of those histologists would likely also assert that for novelty and surprises, the thymus is an awfully good organ to look at in the first place. This is because the thymus was once considered an organ of no great interest, regarded as merely an irregular mass of cells suspended between the heart and the breastbone. However, since those early days, a revolution in understanding about the thymus has taken place, and it is now viewed as perhaps the most important organ helping our bodies to resist disease. The discovery of thymic nurse cells is only one aspect of this ever-growing body of information about this organ.

The feature that sets nurse cells apart from all other cells in the body is that they can "swallow" other cells (lymphocytes) and carry them in their cytoplasm without harming them. A single nurse cell, in fact, may engulf as many as 150 lymphocytes in cytoplasmic vacuoles and release them unharmed upon the appropriate stimulation (see fig. 8). There are approximately 40,000 of these cells scattered throughout the thymus; they seem to envelop some type of immature lymphocyte that amounts to about 3 percent of the total number of lymphocytes found in the organ. Nurse cells are so specialized to do this that they look like no other cells in the body, but it is known that they once were ordinary-looking epithelial cells, since they have the same type of intracellular proteins (e.g., keratin) as do other epithelial cells like skin cells. Nurse cells were only discovered in 1980 by researchers who were trying to break apart the masses of lymphocytes that are present in the thymus. After shaking the thymus apart, many lymphocytes were also separated from each other, but a few were held together in the cytoplasm of nurse cells.

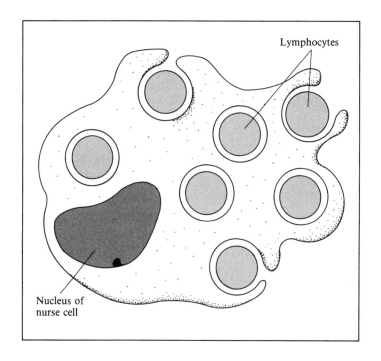

Lymphocytes

Nucleus of
nurse cell

*Figure 8. A thymic nurse cell engulfing
seven circular lymphocytes. This process
appears necessary for complete lymphocyte
development in the thymus.*

Why would nurse cells "swallow" all these lymphocytes, and what significance does this have for the body's fight against disease? The specialized environment within the cytoplasm of thymic nurse cells may help lymphocytes develop into specialized immune system cells. One recent finding about nurse cells is that they contain high concentrations of hormones that are known to affect lymphocyte development.

LYMPHOCYTES

Any "foreign" substance—for example, a virus or a bacterium—that enters the body is termed an *antigen* and is detected and resisted by cells of the immune system. The first step in getting rid of an antigen (fig. 9) is when the antigen somehow sticks to the surface of star-shaped cells called *antigen-presenting cells* that can be found mingled in with lymphocytes in organs such as lymph nodes, the spleen, and in the tonsils. The antigen is probably chemically modified a bit at this stage, and then associates with a membrane protein called the *Ia protein*. The next stage involves a cell that developed in the thymus called a *helper T lymphocyte*. These cells have an unremarkable, spherical appearance, but what makes them interesting are special receptor proteins present in their cell membrane.

Each receptor protein of a T lymphocyte has two regions. One region can attach to the Ia protein of an antigen-presenting cell. The other region is made of protein subunits put together in such a way that the region can assume any one of as many as *10 million* different shapes! If an antigen has the right shape to fit into this highly variable region, and if the other region of the receptor attaches to the Ia protein, then the T lymphocyte explodes into activity. Some T lymphocytes will immediately start searching for and killing any cells in the body infected with the antigen. Other T lymphocytes will stimulate

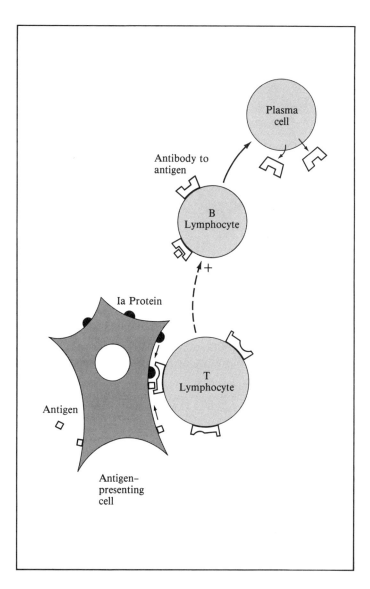

Figure 9. How several cell types in lymphatic organs react to a foreign molecule (antigen).

another type of lymphocyte *(B lymphocytes,* so named because they arise in bone marrow) to take action. They do this by secreting any one of a number of proteins (the interferons) that stimulate B lymphocytes. These B lymphocytes will become *plasma cells* that produce molecules *(antibodies),* which attach to and inactivate the antigen. With the cooperation of both B lymphocytes and T lymphocytes, an invading antigen rarely has a chance of success and is destroyed before much damage can be done.

The importance of T lymphocytes has been dramatically illustrated by the recent rise of *AIDS,* or acquired immune deficiency syndrome. AIDS is now known to be caused by a sexually transmitted virus that enters the body and attaches to a protein called the CD4 protein that is present on the cell membranes of T lymphocytes. The AIDS virus then manages to enter the T cells and kills them. Without T lymphocytes, the immune system becomes severely crippled and is no longer able to fight off disease organisms. As a result, patients afflicted with AIDS acquire secondary infections such as pneumonia, and, for reasons that are not quite clear, may acquire special forms of cancer, causing illness and eventual death. Current research is focusing on the special properties of T cells and of the AIDS virus that may allow a cure for this disease to be found.

What is the role of thymic nurse cells in all this? Nurse cells may play an important role in the development of T lymphocytes in the thymus. In order to function, T cells must "learn" quite a lot during their development in the thymus. T cells must acquire receptors that attach to the Ia protein of antigen-presenting cells. Since nurse cells also have the Ia protein on their surfaces, nurse cells may help "teach" T cells to acquire receptors for the Ia protein. Also, a receptor that will bind to one out of millions of different possible antigens must be devised. When you stop to think of it, this would appear to be an impossible task. It is known that cells have at most 100,000 active genes. How could only this many genes produce 10 million different types of receptors for 10 million different types of T lymphocytes?

In order to accomplish this step, it is now known that the DNA molecules of T cells are actually physically cut and "spliced" to bring the appropriate genes closer together, a procedure unheard of in other cells. Apparently at random, four out of about 1,400 total receptor genes are selected and brought close together during T cell development. Since there are millions of different ways to select and combine only four out of 1,400 genes, the combinations of the proteins that these genes code for can be put together to form the receptor protein complex for many different types of T lymphocytes.

The fully developed immune system of an adult thus has lymphocytes carrying receptors that have almost any possible shape. If an invading "foreign" substance enters the body, the chances are very good that at least one lymphocyte in the body will have a receptor that will attach to the foreign substance, no matter how peculiar its shape may be. What about the DNA for all the other unused genes that are *not* selected to make the receptor for a lymphocyte? Apparently, it is cut away from the chromosomes and thrown away!

Finally, T cells that would attack our own bodily structures and cause harm must be eliminated. This is accomplished by actually killing many thousands of incorrectly formed T cells before they leave the thymus. The ways all these things are accomplished is still not clear. The specialized environment *within* the cytoplasm of thymic nurse cells may bring about some of these changes in the character of T cells. One recent finding about nurse cells is that they contain high concentrations of hormones that are known to affect lymphocyte development. Thus, thymic nurse cells may prove to be important "educators" of developing immune cells.

CHAPTER FIVE
UNUSUAL NERVE CELLS

Because they have such long dendrites and axons, nerve cells must control an enormous volume of cytoplasm. Some nerve cells in the spinal cord, for example, must send axons as far as three feet away from the cell nucleus to innervate a muscle in, say, the foot. Compared to the size of the central portion of the nerve cell, this is a tremendous distance. If a nerve cell were magically enlarged so that its central cell body were as large as a basketball, then such an axon would be almost two miles long! To provide the proteins maintaining so much cytoplasm, nerve cells have unusually abundant amounts of rough endoplasmic reticulum. Another unusual feature of nerve cells is that when they are mature, they lose the ability to undergo mitosis; once again, the reasons for this are not known. However, even after allowing for all these differences from most cells, a few nerve cells stand out as being peculiar.

PURKINJE CELLS

Nerve cells first described by the Czech physiologist Johannes Purkinje (Poor-KIN-ye) in 1837 have one of the most striking shapes of any cell in the body. These cells are located in the cerebellum, a portion of the brain mainly concerned with regulating the posture and movement of the body. Like many nerve cells, they possess an axon, which carries an electrical impulse *away* from the central area of the cell, and also dendrites, which carry impulses *toward* the cell nucleus. The dendrites of a Purkinje cell are what make it appear so specialized. Purkinje cells have a flattened "tree" of dendritic processes that is extraordinarily large, complex, and branched. The diagram of one such dendritic tree, which comprises most of fig. 10, is here actually highly simplified, since many Purkinje cells have a dendritic tree with as many as eight hundred separate segments! Secondly, neighboring Purkinje cells have their fanlike dendritic trees oriented precisely parallel to each other, so that none intersect (fig. 11). Each dendritic tree receives information from other nerve cells in a precise and unique way.

Passing through the dendritic trees of Purkinje cells are axons called *parallel fibers* (dotted lines in fig. 11), which are derived from other cerebellar nerve cells. Information is passed from these axons to the Purkinje cells in a way seen throughout the nervous system, that is,

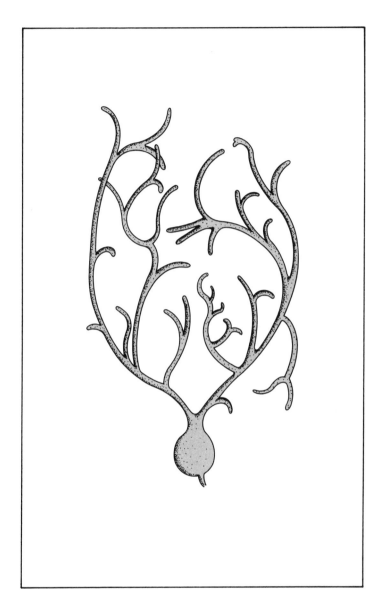

*Figure 10. The Purkinje cell of the
cerebellum has an elaborate fan of dendrites.*

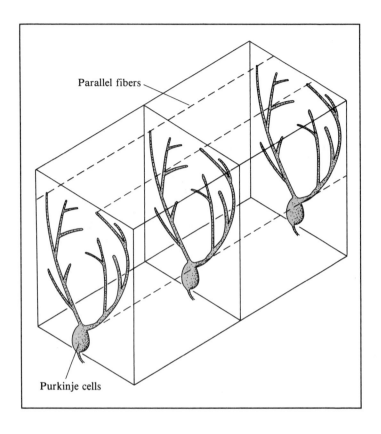

Figure 11. In the cerebellum, Purkinje cells are oriented perpendicularly to long, thin axons of other cells called parallel fibers.

via *synapses*, specialized patches of cell membrane upon an axon.

When an electrical impulse reaches a synapse, it causes membrane proteins to change their shape and allow atoms of calcium to rush into the cytoplasm beneath the synapse. This in turn causes vesicles containing one of many chemicals called *neurotransmitters* to release these chemicals onto the surface of the nearby Purkinje cell dendrite. The neurotransmitter attaches to receptors upon the Purkinje cell, and as a result, causes an electrical impulse to travel in the direction of the Purkinje cell nucleus. This in itself is not unusual; what *is* unusual is that the electrical signal arriving at the base of the dendritic tree is more or less the sum of all the thousands of synaptic inputs impinging upon all of the dendritic processes. Thus, Purkinje cells can integrate the input from thousands of parallel fibers into a single output from the Purkinje cell axon.

What causes the Purkinje cells to develop into such extraordinary nerve cells? One hypothesis, called the *filopodial synaptogenic* (fy-lo-POD-i-al sin-ap-to-GEN-ic) hypothesis, may explain the development of Purkinje cells. During development, Purkinje cells first produce two to three growing processes called *growth cones* (fig. 12). At the tips of each growth cone are small fingerlike processes called filopodia that, like in amoebas and other "crawling" cells, apparently help the cell explore its environment. When a filopodium touches a parallel fiber (diagrammed in cross section as a circle in fig. 12) and makes synaptic contact with it, it enlarges into a growing dendrite; otherwise, it degenerates. Since there are so many parallel fibers around a Purkinje cell, the growth cones make many synapses and turn into a highly branched dendritic tree. This theory

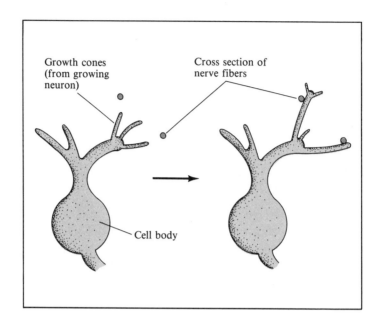

Figure 12. One theory of how Purkinje cells produce their "fan" of dendritic processes. Each time a growing process makes synaptic contact with a parallel fiber (circles in cross section), it enlarges and survives.

seems to account fairly well for the highly branched nature of the Purkinje cell dendritic tree; it fails to explain why each tree is so flat and so precisely parallel to others.

One recent finding in neuroscience that may apply to all growing nerve cells, as well as to Purkinje cells, is the discovery of a special protein, called *growth associated protein-43*, that seems to be found in the dendrites of only neurons that are changing their shape. The suspicion that this protein *causes* the shape change has recently been supported by an ingenious experiment: if this protein is artificially introduced into cultured kidney or connective tissue cells, they will start to behave like neurons and begin to grow long, dendritelike processes! GAP-43 protein may thus interact in some way with membrane proteins that govern cell shape in developing Purkinje cells.

Changes in neuronal shape appear important not only for development but also for another process, the formation of memories in the brain. It has long been suspected that learning and memory formation may involve the production of new connections between nerve cells. A simple example of this would be when we learn to associate the appearance of a candle flame with the painful sensation of a burned finger.

One model of learning would propose that the cells in the visual system of the eye and the brain that perceive the flame form a stronger connection with the nerve cells that communicate sensations of pain to the brain, and thus form a permanent record that a candle flame can be associated with pain. To accomplish this, some long-lasting, anatomical change in connections between nerve cells may take place. It is interesting in this regard that growth associated protein-43 becomes very abundant in areas of the brain activated during learning. More study of this protein may be of aid in finally understanding the mysterious changes in neuronal shape that we think may account for the generation and storage of memories.

One aspect of Purkinje cell development that has attracted much recent interest is its relationship to a brain disorder called *autism*. Autism is a brain disorder that can be recognized in children soon after they are born and causes afflicted children to be withdrawn and unable to respond properly to their environment. Recently, some children suffering from autism have been found to have had impaired development of a certain portion of the cerebellum, perhaps because of an abnormality in Purkinje cell development. Since this area of the cerebellum is connected to other brain areas that regulate things such as responsiveness to sensations, a biological basis for this disorder may thus finally have been found. More study of how these cells develop could shed light upon the origin of the defect in this disorder.

RETINAL PHOTORECEPTOR CELLS

Another highly specialized form of nerve cell is a type of photoreceptor found in the retina of the eye, called a *rod cell* because of its cylindrical shape. The basic task of a rod cell is to detect rays of light that pass through it and to respond by sending an electrical signal to the brain. The entire structure of the cell is modified to accomplish this.

Rod cells can be divided into two segments: one segment (the "inner segment") possesses an axon, a nucleus, and other normal organelles; the other segment ("outer segment") is entirely filled by dozens of hollow, flattened membranous sacs derived from infoldings of the cell membrane (fig. 13). Connecting the two segments is a short stalk; close inspection of the stalk reveals a *basal body* made of microtubules and suggests that the entire outer segment of a rod cell is nothing more than a highly modified cilium! This is not really so surprising in view of the fact that the outer segment of the rod cell is a light-sensing structure, and that cilia of many cells have a sensory function. How does this peculiar-looking cilium actually sense light?

The key to understanding how rod cells work is a special protein called *rhodopsin*. Rhodopsin is a protein composed of 348 amino acids that is attached to the membranes of the flattened sacs, or discs, in the rod outer segment. As a matter of fact, rhodopsin is "threaded" into and out of the disk membrane seven times to form a doughnut-shaped structure with a central pore, rather like the glucose-transporter protein described in chapter 3.

In fig. 13B, an outer segment of a rod cell has been sliced in half to reveal the membranous discs and doughnut-shaped rhodopsin molecules; most of the cytoplasm of the inner segment, connected via a stalk to the outer segment, has been removed in this diagram for greater clarity. The

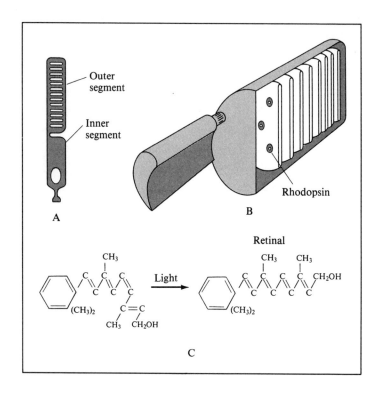

Figure 13. (A) Rod cells respond to light in the retina. (B) Doughnut-shaped molecules of rhodopsin are embedded in many layers of membranous disks within the rod cells. (C) The rhodopsin molecules enable the cell to react to light.

rhodopsin molecule is not a pure protein, but has a form of vitamin A, called *retinal* loosely attached to it (fig. 13C). Retinal readily absorbs light because of its many double bonds between carbon atoms ($C=C$). When light strikes retinal, it causes it to change its shape and to break free from the rhodopsin protein. This is the first step in transforming the energy delivered by light to the rod cell into an electrical response. Rod cells basically operate best in dim light and don't give us very accurate details or information about the colors surrounding us. The task of color vision is carried out by another photoreceptor cell. These color-sensitive cells are similar to rod cells but have a cone-shaped outer segment and so are called *cone cells*. These cells also have membranous discs and a membrane protein much like rhodopsin. Cone cells that respond primarily to red, green, or blue light, however, all have rhodopsin proteins that are slightly different from each other. The amino acids in the region of the protein-binding retinal are different in blue-sensitive cones from those in red-sensitive cones, for example.

This difference in amino acid composition appears to change the electrical charge on the region of the protein close to retinal. Such a difference in electrical charge may influence the absorption of light by retinal and thus may "tune" it to absorb blue, green, or red light preferentially. People suffering from color blindness have cones that function abnormally and thus can't distinguish red colors from other ones of similar intensity. This appears to be due to abnormal rhodopsin proteins in the cones of color blind people.

CHAPTER SIX
THE LIFE AND DEATH OF CELLS

The existence of most cells, like that of higher organisms, eventually ends in death. Yet, the reasons for and mechanisms of cell death are still fundamentally mysterious, although a number of theories have been advanced to explain them. Among these are proposals that death occurs when cells succumb to an ever-growing accumulation of chemical damage to DNA and other cell components that they are no longer able to repair. Others hold that cells are able to renew themselves by cell division for only a fixed number of times, and then die. Still other considerations are whether or not some cells are more long-lived than others, but succumb to the abnormal environment present in the body when one or more organ systems fail.

All these viewpoints regard death as a process that cells resist but eventually cannot prevail over. However, this concept has several flaws. One flaw is that these viewpoints disregard the possibility that cell death is an active process deliberately initiated by cells. Normal development of some tissues *requires* cell death. One example is in the developing limb, in which connective tissue cells between the developing fingers die off to prevent the appearance of a webbed hand instead of a hand with separate fingers. Another example is in the developing brain, where large numbers of nerve cells die if they don't establish proper synaptic connections. These examples of programmed cell death indicate that death at some times may be a planned, active deliberate process. Production by dying cells of some sort of "suicide protein" may perhaps take place, since some cases of programmed cell death can be prevented if chemicals that prevent the synthesis of new proteins are given.

"IMMORTAL" CELLS

Another fact to consider is that some cells appear virtually immortal. Cancer cells, for example, can divide and live almost indefinitely. Normal germ cells, such as the egg cells in the ovary, may reside in the body for forty years, divide after being fertilized thousands of times, and produce daughter cells (more egg cells) in a baby that will repeat the process! Thus, some cells die in the early embryo, whereas others seem to persist indefinitely.

One curious correlation is that cells with only a single set of chromosomes, such as bacterial or sperm and egg cells, often have the capacity to divide and live indefinitely, whereas cells with two sets of chromosomes (most body cells) eventually die. The appearance in evolutionary time of two sets of chromosomes and the ability to engage in sexual reproduction seem to coincide with the appearance of a limited life span and death. Possession of two sets of chromosomes provides an advantage to an organism, because it allows the mixing of genetic material from two individuals by sexual reproduction. Perhaps, however, the sexual mode of reproduction is best for organisms with a limited lifespan, so that the DNA from one individual is removed from the population by death after a while. Death may increase the mixing of DNA and the genetic variability of a population and make it more responsive to evolutionary pressures.

A look at the life and death of a single type of cell may let us examine some of the questions surrounding the death of cells. Some of the reasons underlying cell death have become especially well understood for one type of cell in particular: the red blood cell. Not only the death, but also the unusual life, of these cells is worth looking at.

THE LIFE OF A
RED BLOOD CELL

Red blood cells are disk-shaped cells that make up the vast majority (99 percent) of all the cells carried in the bloodstream. There are a lot of these cells in our bodies: blood makes up about 7 percent of our body weight, and contains a total of about 50 billion red blood cells (about 10 million for each milliliter of blood). A major task of these cells is to absorb oxygen entering the capillaries in the lungs and to carry it to all the cells in the body. Red blood cells carry oxygen in combination with a chemical called *hemoglobin* (HEE-mo-glo-bin), a molecule made up of iron, a compound called *heme* that holds the iron in place, and proteins called *globins*. Hemoglobin has the ideal property of binding to oxygen in an environment where oxygen is abundant, and releasing oxygen in an environment where oxygen is low, and thus serves as a perfect way to deliver oxygen to cells that need it. It is so ideal a compound, in fact, that one wonders why it needs to be carried around in red blood cells at all. Why doesn't the body simply secrete it directly into the bloodstream, like other proteins present in blood?

The simple reason it is necessary to package hemoglobin in blood cells is that it would be impossible to dissolve enough hemoglobin in the blood and still pump it through the heart. If the required hemoglobin were dissolved in blood, blood would get thick and syrupy, or *viscous*, and the heart just wouldn't be strong enough to force blood through blood vessels. Instead hemoglobin is densely packaged in red blood cells, which are just small enough to be transported through the smallest capillaries and which are highly modified to carry as much hemoglobin as possible. Two major modifications make red blood cells highly unusual cells.

The first unusual feature of a red blood cell (RBC) is its shape. Each RBC is shaped like a disc with a hollow scooped out of both sides. Mathematically, this shape provides the greatest amount of surface area possible for a cell of this size and allows the greatest possible exposure of the cell membrane to oxygen in lung capillaries. This shape is maintained by membrane proteins like *spectrin*, which was first discovered in RBCs. The other strange feature of an RBC is its cytoplasm, which, like the cytoplasm of lens cells, contains *no* ribosomes or membranous organelles and which *lacks* a nucleus. Most of the cytoplasm is occupied by hemoglobin, which accounts for a third of the weight of an RBC. What provokes a cell to develop into such a strange specimen, and how can it survive without most of its organelles?

Red blood cells develop in the bone marrow of adults, although in babies and after certain blood diseases, RBCs can also be born in organs such as the spleen and liver. They arise from cells called *erythroblasts* (er-REE-thro-blasts) that undergo a series of changes to become RBCs. To accumulate the components of hemoglobin, erythroblasts make many ribosomes to manufacture globin proteins.

In some people of African descent, the gene that codes for hemoglobin produces a molecule with one incorrect amino acid. This type of hemoglobin still carries oxygen, but in a low oxygen environment aggregates into long crystals inside red blood cells, deforming their shape.

This genetic disorder, called *sickle cell anemia* after the abnormal shape of affected red blood cells, can cause circulatory problems, pain, and even death. Knowledge of the molecular basis of this disorder may make some form of treatment possible.

As erythroblasts develop further, they acquire many transferrin receptors in the cell membrane so that iron can be brought into the cell (see chapter 4). A final step in development occurs when the cytoplasm pinches into two portions, one portion containing primarily the nucleus, and then divides in half to discard the nucleus. In animals such as birds, reptiles, and amphibians, RBCs fail to take this last drastic step in development and retain their nuclei; this would seem to make these RBCs less efficient as pure carriers of hemoglobin, but this may perhaps be permissible in animals with a metabolic rate, and an oxygen demand lower than our own.

Once an RBC is formed, its life is severely restricted by the simplicity of its structure. It cannot combine nutrients with oxygen because it lacks mitochondria; it cannot make new proteins because it lacks rough endoplasmic reticulum. This latter limitation is what leads to the death of the cell.

Like most cells, RBCs have abundant amounts of a bicarbonate channel protein called *band 3* in their cell membranes (see chapter 3). This protein is vulnerable to attack by chemicals such as glucose, which is present in the blood and after a while (about 120 days for most red blood cells) becomes abnormal or deformed as a consequence of this chemical attack. This dooms the RBC to destruction, for cells of the immune system will no longer recognize the band 3 protein as belonging to the body and will treat it as a foreign antigen. B-type *lymphocytes* (immune system cells), for example, will react to the abnormal band 3 protein and produce antibodies that bind to it. The RBC will become coated with a layer of antibodies in a process called *opsonization* (op-son-i-ZAY-shun). This has no immediate consequences; however, once the RBC enters the spleen, it is headed for trouble.

Once in the spleen an opsonized RBC will encounter a *macrophage*, (MAK-ro-faj). At this time, the macrophage will react to destroy the RBC. The antibodies coating the RBC surface will attach to receptors for antibodies located on the macrophage cell membrane, and the macrophage will respond by "swallowing" or *phagocytizing* (FAY-go-si-tie-zing) the RBC until the cytoplasm of the macrophage totally surrounds it (fig. 14).

Inside the macrophage destructive enzymes are carried by membranous cytoplasmic vesicles called *lysosomes* (LY-so-somes) to the engulfed RBC, and it is gradually destroyed. Finally, all that remains of the RBC are residual deposits of degraded hemoglobin and iron in the cytoplasm of the macrophage.

Does this process apply to the death of all cells? Perhaps, since abnormal band 3 protein can

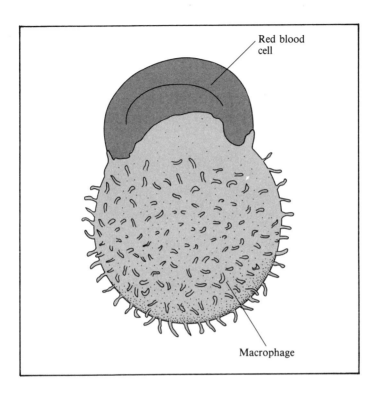

Red blood
cell

Macrophage

*Figure 14. A red blood cell that
has become aged and abnormal. A
macrophage engulfs and destroys it.*

be detected on other types of aging cells. However, unlike RBCs, most other cells are constantly recycling and renewing their cell membranes by pinching off membranous vesicles, moving them around the cytoplasm, and fusing them to the cell membrane again. Presumably, during this process, called *membrane flow*, the cell has some way of recognizing and destroying abnormal patches of membrane. Some explanation for a failure to do this, as well as for a failure to regulate other cell processes, would have to be found to explain why most cells die and are destroyed.

A FINAL WORD

Many other examples come to mind of cells that undergo fantastic changes in structure to perform a function. Often, one aspect of a cell alone is disproportionately expanded to fulfill a task. In a skin cell, for example, the cytoskeletal protein keratin is so grossly overproduced that the cell becomes totally filled with keratin and acts as a water repellent "shingle" covering over the skin. Mast cells become filled with tremendous amounts of histamine so that they can expel this chemical onto blood vessels during an allergic reaction (and in doing so make our eyes red and watery!). Plasma cells acquire huge stacks of endoplasmic reticulum that allow the cells to act as antibody-producing "factories."

How cells are able to accomplish these transformations is likely to be a continuing source of fascination in the foreseeable future for those of us interested in biology. New techniques of cell biology, by allowing us to decipher the structures of more and more proteins every month, are likely to provide the tools to solve these questions at an unprecedented rate. The new insights into cell function we have looked at in these pages are just the beginning of what is to come.

GLOSSARY

Amino acid. One of twenty-three naturally occurring compounds in the body that all contain an acid molecule ($COOH$) on one end and an amino molecule (NH_2) on the other end. Amino acids can be linked to form long chains (proteins) by joining acid molecules to amino molecules.

Antibodies. Y-shaped protein molecules produced by cells of the immune system (lymphocytes). Each antibody can bind to foreign molecules (antigens) having only one specific shape.

Bacterium. Simple type of cell that lacks a nucleus and which may cause disease.

Bases. Chemical compounds (guanine, adenine, cytosine, or thymine) arranged in a long series, forming the genetic "code," in DNA or RNA.

Capillary. The smallest type of blood vessel, usually leaky to allow exchange of molecules between tissues and the bloodstream.

Cell. The smallest unit of independent life.

Cell membrane. A watertight film of oil and proteins that encloses a cell.

Chromosomes. Long molecules of DNA that become smaller, denser, and, hence, visible during cell division.

Cilia. Tubular projections from the cell membrane that may be moved or used as sensors.

Cytoplasm. Watery material between the cell nucleus and membrane that contains the cell's nutrients, products, and organelles.

DNA. Deoxyribonucleic acid, the genetic material in a cell.

Endocrine cells. Cells that produce proteins or steroids as hormones that are conveyed to other parts of the body via the bloodstream.

Endoplasmic reticulum. A complicated network of membranes within a cell involved in the synthesis of proteins and other products.

Enzyme. A protein molecule that can promote specific chemical reactions within cells.

Epithelial cells. Cells that are tightly joined together to form hollow structures (capillaries, ducts) or to cover surfaces (skin).

Exocrine cells. Cells that produce proteins *(e.g.,* enzymes) and convey them to another part of the body via ducts.

Gene. A portion of chromosomal DNA that contains the information needed to make a specific protein, which may form the basis for genetic differences between individuals.

Glucose. The type of sugar resulting from digestion of many foods; used as a main source of energy for many cells.

Hormone. A molecule carried throughout the bloodstream that affects cell function.

Lymphocytes. Cells of the immune system dedicated to the detection and destruction of invading, foreign substances such as disease-causing bacteria.

Micron. Unit of measurement: 1/1000 of a millimeter.

Mitochondria. Tubular or bean-shaped organelles that provide energy to operate cells.

Molecules. Combinations of atoms that form nutrients, proteins, etc.

Nucleus. The largest cell organelle, surrounded by two membranes and containing the chromosomes.

Organelles. Cell components composed of many molecules of proteins or lipids that carry out one or more cell functions.

Protein. Long molecule composed of a series of amino acids joined together; can function as part of a cell structure or as an enzyme controlling chemical reactions.

Receptors. Protein molecules, often embedded in the cell membrane, that can attach to and respond to molecules floating in the environment around the cell.

Retina. Layer of cells inside the eyeball that is responsive to light.

Ribosomes. Small aggregations of protein and RNA that manufacture proteins.

RNA. Ribonucleic acid.

Tissue. Aggregation of basically similar cells performing a definite function in a portion of an organ. Four basic types are epithelial, nervous, muscular, and connective.

Vesicle. Fluid-filled "bubble" inside cells formed from an infolding of the cell membrane. May often contain specific proteins or contents that will be transported to a specific place within the cell.

FOR FURTHER READING

Alberts, B. *Molecular Biology of the Cell.* New York: Garland, 1989.

Clark, G. *History of Staining.* Baltimore: Williams & Wilkins, 1983.

De Kruif, Paul. *Microbe Hunters.* San Diego: Harcourt Brace, Jovanovich, 1966.

Dronamraju, K.R. *The Foundations of Human Genetics.* Springfield, Ill.: C.C. Thomas, 1989.

Lehrer, S. *Explorers of the Body.* New York: Doubleday, 1979.

Portugal, F.H. *A Century of DNA.* Cambridge: MIT Press, 1977.

Watson, J.D. *The DNA Story.* San Francisco: W. H. Freeman, 1981.

INDEX

ABOUT THE AUTHOR

John K. Young is associate professor of anatomy at Howard University in Washington, D.C. This book grew out of nine years of experience in teaching microscopic anatomy to medical and dental students who, he says, "provoked me by numerous questions to find out, in as much detail as is known, how exactly cells in various parts of the body work." Dr. Young is married and has two sons. His hobbies include bicycle riding, music, and Russian and German literature.